THIS WALKER BOOK BELONGS TO:

_____

_____

_____

_____

For Josie and Oliver

First published 1995 by Walker Books Ltd
87 Vauxhall Walk, London SE11 5HJ

This edition published 1997

4 6 8 10 9 7 5 3

© 1995 Lucy Cousins

Hand lettering by Lucy Cousins

Printed in Hong Kong/China

British Library Cataloguing in Publication Data
A catalogue record for this book is
available from the British Library.

ISBN 0-7445-4764-4

Za-Za's
Baby Brother

Lucy Cousins

WALKER BOOKS
AND SUBSIDIARIES
LONDON · BOSTON · SYDNEY

My mum is going to have a baby.

She has a big fat tummy. There's not much room for a cuddle.

Granny came to look after me.

Dad took mum to the hospital.

When the baby was born we went to see mum.

When Mum came home
she was Very tired.
I had to be very quiet
and help Dad
look after
her.

All my uncles and aunts came to see the baby.

hat a
good
boy

ooh he's
gorgeous

I played on
my own.

Dad was always busy.

Mum was always busy.

"Dad, will you read me a story?"
"Not now, Za-za. We're going shopping soon."

"Mum, can we go to the toyshop?"

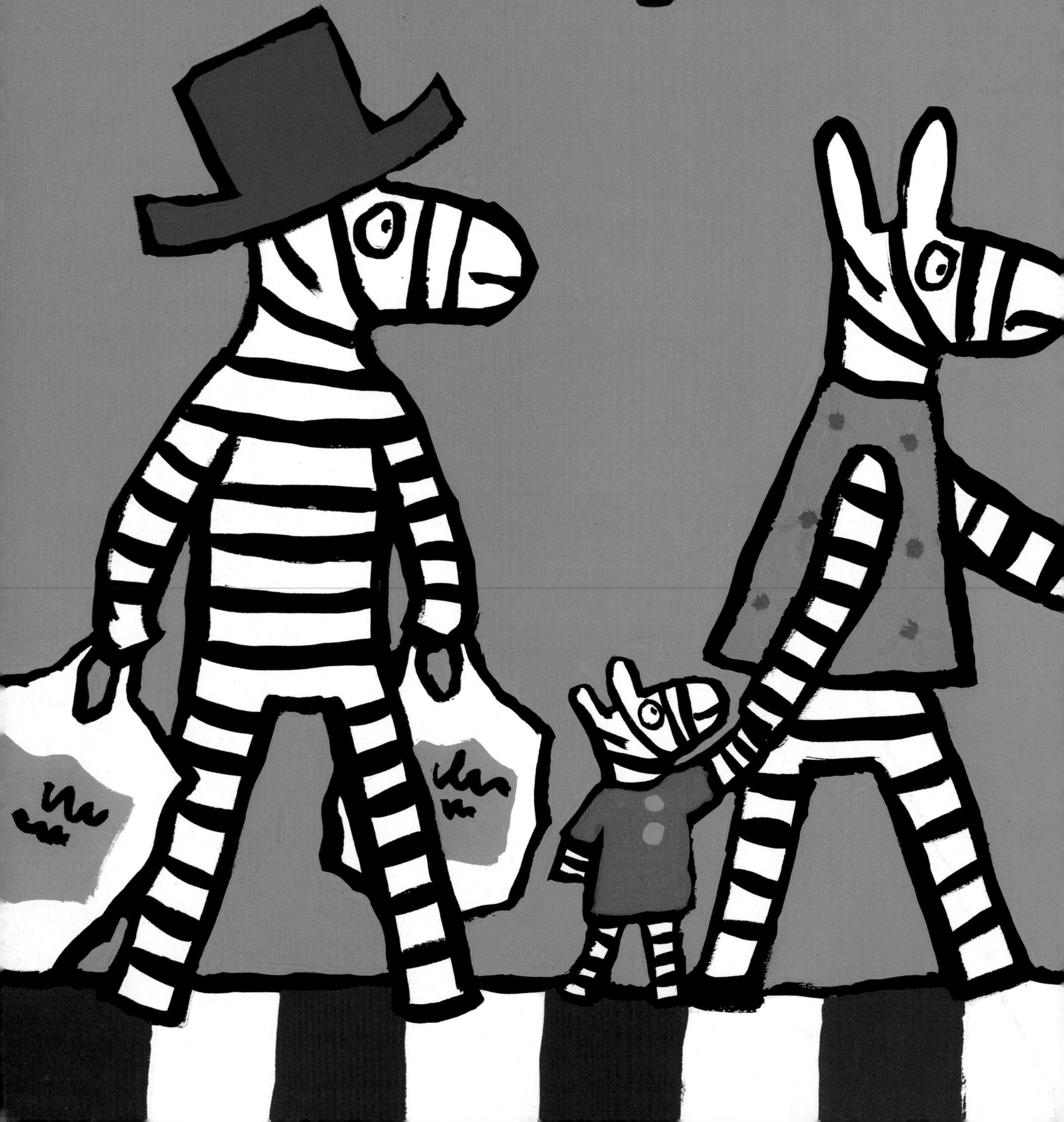

"Sorry, Za-za, baby's hungry and we have to go home."

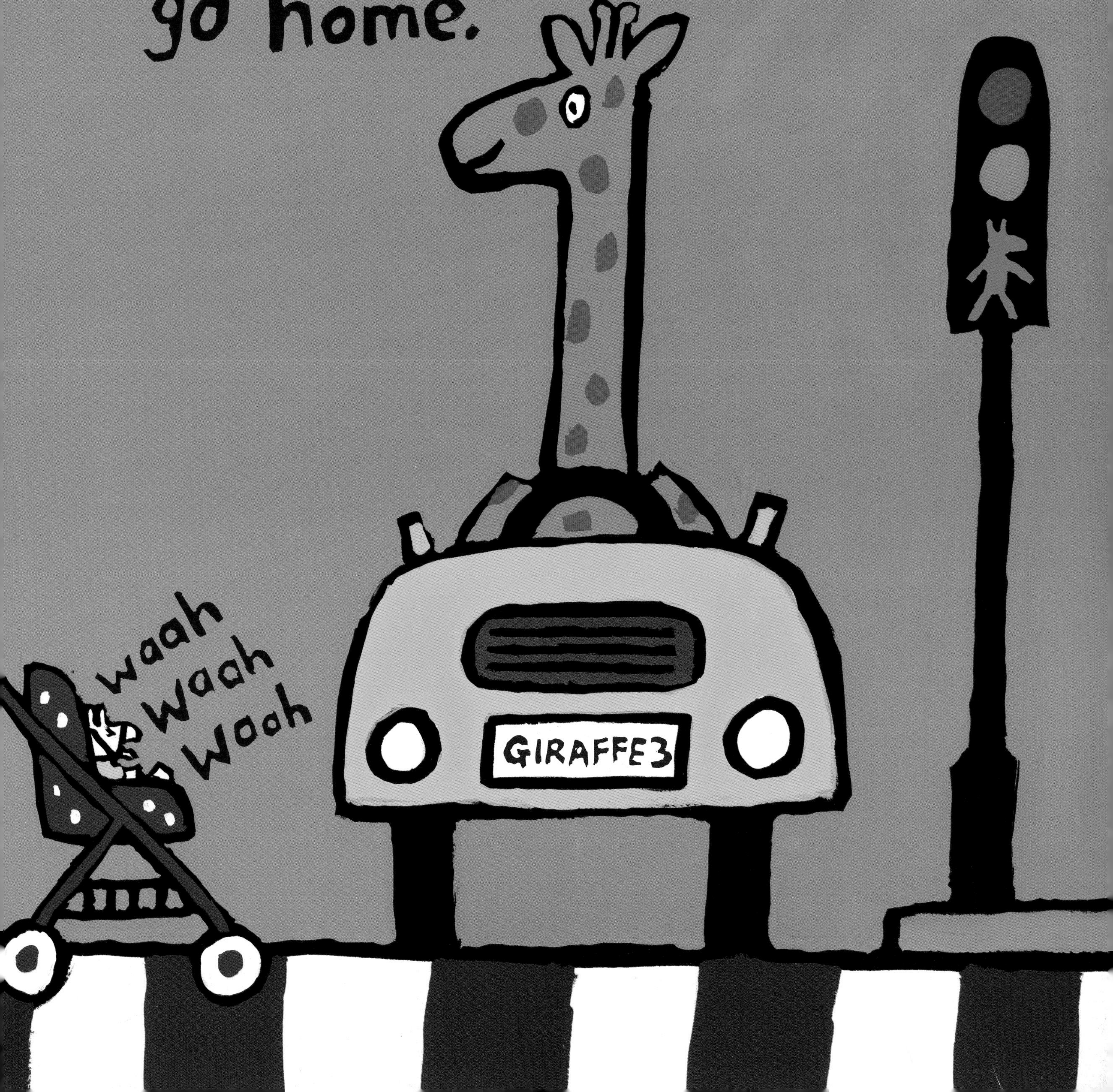

"Can I have my tea soon?"

"Yes, Za-za."

So I cuddled the baby...

and I pushed him...

and I
built him
a tower.

He was nice.
It was fun.

When the baby got tired Mum put him to bed.

Then I got my cuddle...

and a bedtime story.

MORE WALKER PAPERBACKS
For You to Enjoy

NOAH'S ARK
by Lucy Cousins

"Filled with a rainbow of bold, eye-catching illustrations which leap from the pages, this fine retelling of the Noah's Ark story will enchant youngsters." *Practical Parenting*

0-7445-3672-3   £4.99

PINKY THE RABBIT
by Lucy Cousins

Pinky, the rabbit, can see creatures in the hedge, the pond, the grass… He can hear noises in the flowers, the trees, the sky… Small children will have lots of fun guessing what's hidden beneath the flaps in these colourful novelty books by the creator of Maisy, the mouse.

"Marvellous, bold, bright, very direct. For very young children … an absolute winner." *Tony Bradman, BBC Radio's Treasure Islands*

What Can Pinky See?   0-7445-4931-0
What Can Pinky Hear?   0-7445-4930-2

£4.99 each

MOUSE PARTY
by Alan Durant/Sue Heap

A cat with a mat, a giraffe with a bath, a hen with a pen – these are just some of the guests at Mouse's house-warming party. But then an elephant arrives and claims the house is his! A simple rhyming text and bright, funny illustrations make this a great picture book for young children.

"Readers will want to rave on with this one until they drop." *The Observer*

0-7445-4390-8   £4.50